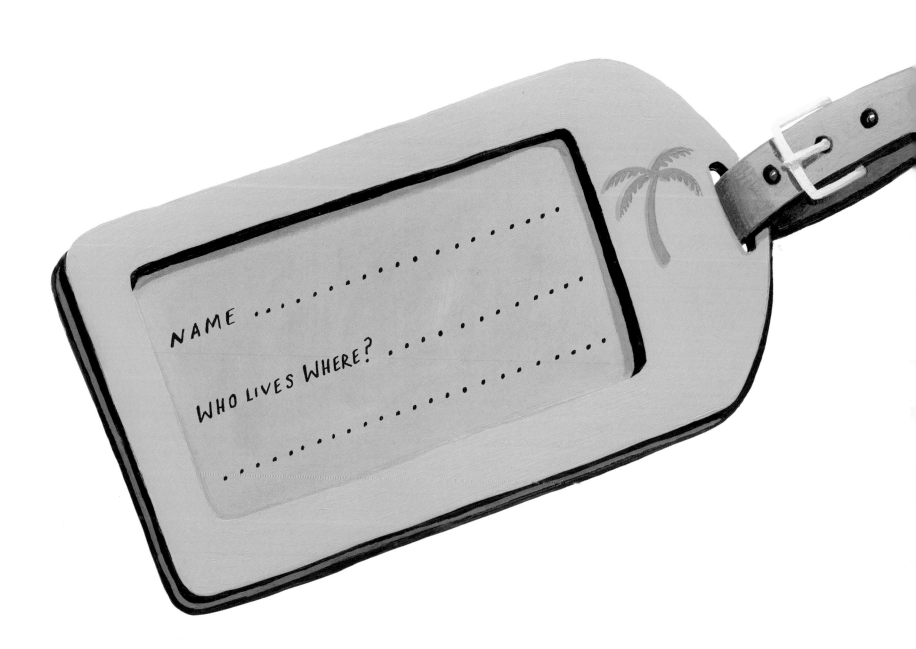

For Penny – J.H.
For Kyle – G.P.

First published 2021 by Macmillan Children's Books
an imprint of Pan Macmillan
The Smithson, 6 Briset Street, London, EC1M 5NR
Associated companies throughout the world
www.panmacmillan.com

ISBN: 978-1-5290-2628-3 (PB)
ISBN: 978-1-5290-5216-9 (EB)

Text copyright © John Hay 2021
Illustration copyright © Garry Parsons 2021

9 8 7 6 5 4 3 2 1

A CIP catalogue record for this book is
available from the British Library.

Printed in China.

"YOU LIVE WHERE?!"

JOHN HAY AND
GARRY PARSONS

MACMILLAN CHILDREN'S BOOKS

It was the first day of the holiday and down by the pool the birds were all getting to know each other.

"Where do you come from?"
a kookaburra asked the roadrunner
on the next lounger.

"Nowhere," replied the roadrunner.

"But you must live somewhere."

"I do. I live in **NOWHERE**. Lived there all my life. There's nowhere quite like **NOWHERE**."

RUNNER'S WORLD

"Actually," said a little penguin,
"there is somewhere like **NOWHERE**.
Because I live near **NOWHERE ELSE!**"

"Well, that's just silly,"
said the kookaburra.

"No, I'm from **SILLY**," said a jackdaw, "and I'm hungry. Can I get some toast?"

"TOAST?"
asked a woodpecker.
"I just came from there."

"Okay," sighed the kookaburra. "Anyone else from a place with a funny name?"

"Ooh," hooted a barn owl. "You could say I came from an egg – from **EGG!**"

Across the pool, a couple of herons were relaxing on their sun loungers. "Shhh!" said one. "My friend's trying to sleep."

"And where do you live?" asked the kookaburra.

"LITTLE SNORING."

"And your friend? No, let me guess . . . Great Snoring?"

"Don't be daft. He lives in SCRATCHY BOTTOM."

"THAT'S ENOUGH!"
said the kookaburra.

"If I hear one more silly
name . . ."

"Fair enough," said a chicken. "Let's all calm down. May I introduce myself? I'm a chicken, and I come from DUCK."

"And I'm a duck, and I come from CHICKEN!"

"I SAID NO MORE SILLY NAMES!"

said the kookaburra.

"*Uh-oh*," said a cuckoo.
"I think somebody must live in **MISERY**.
Or maybe even in **ANGER**."

"Yes, why are you
so grumpy?" asked
a hummingbird.
"I thought kookaburras
were always laughing?"

"I'm not a laughing kookaburra. I'm a blue-winged kookaburra, from the sensible side of the family. And where are you from, anyway?"

"I'm from **DINOSAUR**," said the hummingbird, "so you'd better watch out!"

"*Uh-oh*," said the cuckoo. "I'm from **MONSTER**, so don't mess with me."

"And I'm from **POO**, so definitely don't mess with me!" said a red-headed bullfinch.

"Lovely place," said a whooping crane. "Much nicer than where I'm from."

"Really?" said the bullfinch. "Where's that, then?"

"PEE PEE TOWN," said the crane.

A curlew hopped out of the pool and wrapped a towel round herself.

"No peeping," she grinned, "but I come from PANTYFALLEN."

"Honestly, I'm beginning to wish
I'd stayed at home," said the kookaburra.
"Somewhere nice and quiet and with
a proper, serious name."

"And you live . . . where?"
asked the hummingbird.

By now, all the birds were laughing.
Even the kookaburra started chuckling.

There was so much noise
that a local meadowlark
peeked over the fence to
see what was going on.

"Wow, what brings you
lot here?" she asked.

"We just thought it sounded like a fun place for a holiday," said the kookaburra.

"YOU LIVE WHERE?!"

Bird: Roadrunner
Lives in: Nowhere, Oklahoma, USA. If you're passing Nowhere, visit the general store. You can buy a t-shirt so your friends will know you've been to Nowhere!

Bird: Barn Owl
Lives in: Egg, Austria. This village in Austria is famous for its dairy farms. Some of the tastiest cheese in the world comes from Egg!

Bird: Little Penguin
Lives in: Nowhere Else, Tasmania, Australia. Actually, the little penguin lives on the coast near Nowhere Else in a town called Penguin. But that's not a funny name, is it?

Bird: Heron
Lives in: Little Snoring, England. It's true: not only is there a Little Snoring, there's a Great Snoring nearby too. And Little Snoring is bigger than Great Snoring.

Bird: Jackdaw
Lives in: Silly, Belgium. Silly is named after a stream called Sille. There used to be a very old windmill in Silly, but the wind blew it down.

Bird: Heron
Lives in: Scratchy Bottom, England. Scratchy Bottom is a quiet valley. It's a lovely place for a walk, but if you're itching to sit down, maybe go somewhere else.

Bird: Woodpecker
Lives in: Toast, North Carolina, USA. It's said that this town was not named after a tasty snack, but after a pair of shoes, which were a toasty shade of brown. Chewy!

Bird: Chicken
Lives in: Duck, North Carolina, USA. Every year, thousands of ducks stop off in this little town on their way south for the winter. It's not surprising the postmaster named it Duck.

Bird: Duck
Lives in: Chicken, Alaska, USA. The locals decided to name their town after the most common local bird. Ptarmigan. Only no one could spell that, so they called it Chicken instead.

Bird: Hummingbird
Lives in: Dinosaur, Colorado, USA. Dinosaur gets its name from fossils discovered nearby. Would you like to live in Triceratops Terrace or Brontosaurus Boulevard? They're real streets in Dinosaur!

Bird: Cuckoo
Lives in: Monster, Netherlands. Monster might be named after a scary creature that steals people's fries, or it may be from the Old Dutch word for a Big Church . . . which is Monster!

Bird: Red-headed Bullfinch
Lives in: Poo, India. Poo is known for its beautiful scenery and the apricots, grapes and almonds which grow there. Visitors often say how nice Poo smells!

Bird: Whooping Crane
Lives in: Pee Pee Township, Ohio, USA. Years ago, a man named Peter Patrick settled here and carved his initials into a tree. So they named the town after him. Why didn't they just call it Pete?

Bird: Curlew
Lives in: Pantyfallen, Wales. Pantyfallen means 'the valley with the apple tree' in Welsh. So if you see an apple tree in a Welsh valley, hold on to your pants.

Bird: Blue-winged Kookaburra
Lives in: Humpty Doo, Australia. If you go to Humpty Doo, watch out for a giant crocodile wearing boxing gloves! (Luckily The Big Boxing Croc is a local landmark, not a real crocodile.)

Boring, Oregon, USA and **Dull, Scotland.** To celebrate their pairing, Boring and Dull have declared August 9th to be the annual Boring and Dull Day. With ice cream, hot dogs and bagpipes. So not boring and dull after all.